My Favorite Time of Year

Susan Pearson   illustrated by John Wallner

SCHOLASTIC INC.

New York Toronto London Sydney Auckland

For Kelly and Patrick
S. P.

For Jane and Ann Blakemore
J. C. W.

ISBN 0-590-46353-5

Text copyright © 1988 by Susan Pearson.
Illustrations copyright © 1988 by John Wallner.
All rights reserved. Published by Scholastic Inc.,
730 Broadway, New York, NY 10003, by arrangement with
HarperCollins Publishers.

12 11 10 9 8 7 6 5 4 3 2 1   2 3 4 5 6 7/9

Printed in the U.S.A.   09

First Scholastic printing, September 1992

It's October!

The maple trees are turning red.
The elms are turning yellow.
When Kelly and Mommy take baby Patrick for a walk,
they stretch their necks back
to see the colored roof above them:
red and orange and yellow and brown.
"We must look like baby birds," says Mommy.

Then the leaves start to fall,
whirling, swirling in the wind,
landing in one place, then blowing to another.
Kelly chases them everywhere they go,
then brings some in to show to Patrick.
"Now we have fall both outdoors and in!" Mommy says.

Suddenly everyone is busy.

Ms. Marlow is putting up her storm windows.

Mr. Gordon is fixing his roof.

The Zuckermans are covering their roses with straw.

Everyone is buttoning up for winter.
Kelly is playing harder, running faster.
The days are getting shorter.
"There's no time for being slow," says Kelly.

Daddy rakes the leaves, and Kelly jumps into the piles,
sometimes crunchy, sometimes wet, always smelling delicious.
Then Daddy and Kelly march into the kitchen,
where Mommy is making soup and cocoa and steaming up the windows.
Patrick bounces in his swing and laughs.

One day Mommy hears the geese.
"Quick!" she calls and grabs Kelly's hand.
They run outside, forgetting their coats, forgetting even Patrick,
in their hurry to wave good-bye.

Ears of corn go up on doors.
Then jack-o'-lanterns appear on doorsteps.
"Halloween is just around the corner," says Daddy.
"Fall is my favorite time of year!" says Kelly.

It's December!
Kelly makes footprints in the morning frost.
Her breath makes clouds.

"Will it snow today?" she asks every morning.
At last it does.
"It's just spitting," Mommy says at first.
"Nothing to get excited about."
But the flakes get bigger, wetter.
"It's coughing now," Kelly tells Mommy then.
Soon the sky is like a thick, gray blanket
dropping a white blanket on the ground.

Now dressing Patrick seems to take forever.
Sometimes it takes forever twice.
The doorway is filled with snowsuits and scarves,
hats and mittens and boots.
"We look like a department store," says Kelly.

Daddy takes Kelly sledding.
He sits in back and she sits in front, safe between his legs.
Down the hill they fly, the wind whooshing in their ears,
the snow spraying in their faces.

Mommy and Kelly build a snowman.
The snowman wears Daddy's fishing hat and the necktie Mommy hates,
and he carries a mop.
Later Mommy and Kelly hide behind the curtains
to see the look on Daddy's face
when he comes home from work and meets their snowman.

Every morning Mommy and Kelly scatter birdseed
for the birds who have stayed behind.
At night Daddy builds a fire in the fireplace.
It crackles while he reads a story.
Patrick snoozes on a quilt on the floor.
Daisy, their puppy, sleeps by the fire, dreaming of bones.

Soon Santas appear on every corner, ringing bells.
"Which one is really him?" asks Kelly.

The house fills up with the smell of cookies and a feeling of secrets.
Christmas is coming.
"I like winter best of all!" says Kelly.

The brave crocuses know first.
All alone, they push up through the snow.
Then Kelly knows too.
"It's spring!" she says.

Soon the snow melts.
One day Mommy says,
"Look at the secrets that old snow has been keeping!"
Patrick's blue mitten, Kelly's truck, and
the glove Daddy thought he had left on the bus
are not lost anymore.

Suddenly there are puddles everywhere.
Kelly wears her red rubber boots
and splashes wherever she goes.

Mommy spots the first robin.

"Hello, Robin Redbreast," she says. "Welcome back, Spring!"

"Will he build a nest in our tree?" asks Kelly.

"If we're lucky," Mommy tells her.

And then the daffodils are blooming,
all yellow and laughing.
Next the tulips.
So much color surprises everyone, especially Patrick.

The trees are no longer winter sticks.
First they grow tiny buds.
Then the buds open, just a little at first.
"Look, Kelly," says Mommy, "the trees have grown lace."

A few days later, the lace has turned into leaves.
"This is the greenest green," says Kelly.
"We've ever seen," says Mommy.

One day Mommy starts folding snowsuits
and packing them into a trunk.
"We won't need these anymore," she says.
"It won't take so long to dress you," Kelly explains to Patrick.
"Spring is my favorite time of year."

Yesterday Kelly wore overalls.
Today she's wearing shorts.
Daddy takes off his shirt to mow the lawn.
Even the freshly cut grass seems to sweat.
It's summer!

In June Mommy picks lettuce and radishes from the garden.

In July she has peppers and cucumbers as well.

Then in August the tomatoes ripen.

"Summer is like one long salad," says Kelly.

One night, like magic, the fireflies appear.

Daddy pokes holes in the lids of old mayonnaise jars.

Then he and Kelly run around the yard,

catching fireflies to make lanterns.

On Saturdays, like ants in a line,
everyone goes to the beach.
Patrick is walking now, and trying to talk.
Kelly shows him how to dig.
"We are digging to China," she tells him.
" 'Na!" says Patrick.

At suppertime, the whole block smells
of hot dogs and hamburgers cooking on grills.
Kelly's backyard fills with aunts and uncles and cousins.
Daisy races from one to another, barking and wagging her tail.

Before supper, everyone plays horseshoes and croquet.
After supper, they have contests to see
who can spit watermelon seeds the farthest.
Crazy Daisy tries to chase the seeds.

When Kelly's bedtime comes, it is still almost light.
Her windows are open.
She can hear the hum of grown-ups talking on the porch
and big kids still playing down the street.
"Summer is my favorite time of year," she tells her bear.
Then crickets and frogs sing her to sleep.